*For my grandma,*
*who brought comfort and joy to so many hearts,*
*and who made every season bright —J. R.*

*For my grandmother Renate —R. K.*

Farrar Straus Giroux Books for Young Readers • An imprint of Macmillan Publishing Group, LLC • 120 Broadway, New York, NY 10271 • Text copyright © 2022 by Jessica Redman • Illustrations copyright © 2022 by Ramona Kaulitzki • All rights reserved • Color separations by Bright Arts (H.K.) Ltd. • Printed in China by RR Donnelly Asia Printing Solutions Ltd., Dongguan City, Guangdong Province • First edition, 2022 • ISBN 978-0-374-31460-6 (hardcover) • 10 9 8 7 6 5 4 3 2 1 • mackids.com • Library of Congress Cataloging-in-Publication Data is available • Our books may be purchased in bulk for promotional, educational, or business use. Please contact your local bookseller or the Macmillan Corporate and Premium Sales Department at (800) 221-7945 ext. 5442 or by email at MacmillanSpecialMarkets@macmillan.com.

The art for this book was created digitally using Adobe Photoshop. The text was set in Chronicle Text G1 Roman and Garden Pro, and the display type was set in Skate. Designed by Melisa Vuong, with art direction by Aram Kim. Production was supervised by Celeste Cass, and the production editors were Kat Kopit and Helen Seachrist. Edited by Janine O'Malley, with support from Melissa Warten.

# Season of Light

By Jess Redman   Illustrated by Ramona Kaulitzki

Farrar Straus Giroux

New York

After red and green dreams,
We wake up before the sun.
We're counting down December days
But savoring each one.

DECEMBER

1 2 3 4 5 6
7 8 9 10 11 12 13
14 15 16 17 18 19 20
21 22 23 24 25 26 27
28 29 30 31

This is a season of *joy*.

Snowflakes from paper
Sheep and wise men arranged

Glass balls, garlands, stockings
All is magical and changed.

This is a season of *wonder*.

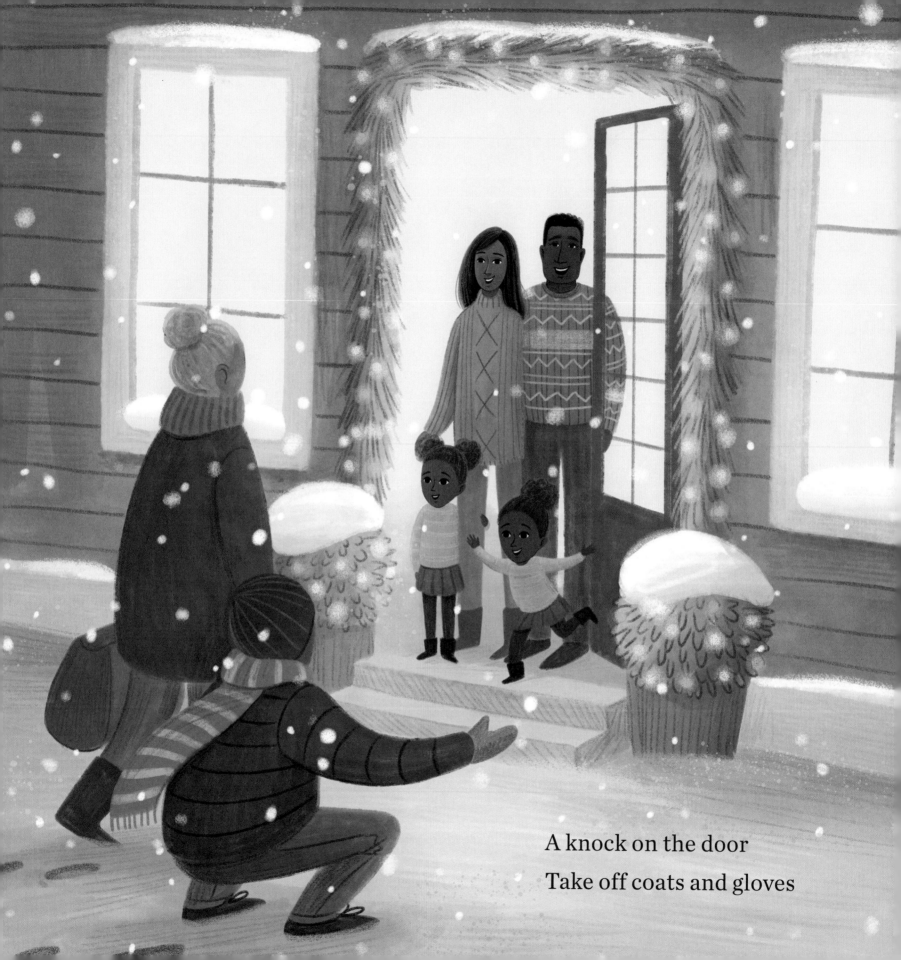

A knock on the door
Take off coats and gloves

A hug, a kiss, a welcome back
Home is where there's love.

This is a season of *together*.

Gifts to wrap and tie

A table to prepare

Open hearts and open hands
All we have is ours to share.

This is a season of *giving*.

Our voices ring out
Silver bells and midnights clear

First noels and glorious morns
Offerings of goodwill and cheer.

This is a season of *song*.

Then gathering to listen
Memories, verses, old and new

Comfort and joy,
    travelers and stars,
Miracles and reindeer, too.

This is a season of *Story*.

Bathrobes and tinsel halos

Now we are part of the story

We come to the stable, visit the manger

We are the angels singing out, "Glory!"

This is a season of *faith*.

Under star-filled winter skies
With homes and trees aglow
With candles lit and hearts so full
Brightness inside, above, and below.

This is a season of *light*.

This is a time to set apart

A time to give and receive.

This is a time to notice and marvel
A time to hear and believe.

And though seasons don't last forever

And the world may not always shine so bright

We can carry Christmas inside us.

We can live a lifetime of light.